the giver in me honors the giver in you.
xo. adrian michael

giver.

giver.
III

adrian michael

a lovasté project
in partnership with hwttbtw
published by
creative genius
CONCORDHAUS

Published by Creative Genius Publishing—
an imprint of lovasté

| Denver, CO | Concord, CA |

To contact the author visit adrianmichaelgreen.com
To see more of the author's work visit IG @adrianmichaelgreen
Book jacket designed by Adrian Michael Green

ISBN-13: 9798615419034

Printed in the United States of America

for the givers.
for those against hate.

a playlist*

fields x giveon
trigger protection mantra x jhené aiko
what you want x chrishan + og parker
got it good x kaytranada + craig david
somebody should kiss you x teddy swims
let me x tone smith
golden hour x kacey musgraves
alluring x guustavv
burning wings x smithfield
swé x mus
ocean eyes x billie eilish
do better x stormzy
nothing without you x the weeknd
find myself x zach karl
sunshine x leilani wolfgramm
firewater x amythyst kiah
do it x chloe + halle
lost & found x trey songz
no filter x jc + jacquees
marigold x dave james + ari lennox + mannywellz
meant to be x bebe rexha + florida georgia line
one more x sg lewis + nile rodgers
i miss you x jax jones +au/ra
old soul x bruno major
until the end of time x justin timberlake + beyoncé
asé x junius paul

incense. palo santo. candles. sage.
tea. whiskey. wine. water. beer.

*to be listened to. lit and sipped while reading or between readings for ultimate experience.

make waves.

this volume)my hope(is that it feels different. feels intimate. feels personal. as if i am speaking to you. in front of you. laid out. reaching. as if i know exactly what you need before you say anything. this is for the dreamers. the ones who play out over and over in their minds what they need but find it really hard once they open their eyes. this is one long letter. curated and mailed to your attention. your name here _____.
i know sometimes you want to turn to call to text to face to meet to say what needs to be said. and when you breathe out there is always a missing piece to how you are received. how your words land. it isn't quite soul understood. people hear what you say but really can't relate. they want to. but it is different when it is someone who is a master of empathy. many fail to tap into that realm. they try. but say the wrong things back. don't know what to say and accidentally make matters worse. but this one. this one. this one. this third installment. is for the star in you. the dimmest one. the furthest one. that part of you that tries not to make waves. that part of you that needs flag. that needs marker. that needs water. your water. to capsize you. to home you. to breathe you in one long long long deep deep deep sigh in and in and out and out. to grant you. to permit you. to encourage you. to flow as you flow and spill where you spill. as it is your pour)your overflooding pour(that is what has sustained sustained sustained sustained others and too many times you are at your last but even your last is full and you shouldn't have to always save you for last. this one is to save you for first. for you to come up and stay up and freshen. you are beyond the word precious that is just a placeholder. somewhere in here please grab hold of a word a phrase a passage a meter a feeling to take you to where you have been missing. back into you. into your love that anyone anyone anyone would beg for.

sometimes the healing hurts more than the loss itself.

sometimes the healing hurts more than the loss itself. and in that pain in that wound in that space of most difficulty you can find yourself grabbing at straws. grabbing at nothing. sobbing for recovery. craving to undo the loss. to undue the grueling. the agony the agony is not see-through. the harsh the harsh is thick and lonely and not understandable. but. but. breathe. remember who you are and that it is okay to be down for what you wish to have had much longer. but in the healing. in the mourning. in the difficulty the hurting tells you what to do. how to move. how to feel. how to figure. breathe to it. beat to it. acknowledge it don't block it or it will keep visiting with the same frequency. so when it visits. when it circles. when it drains. tell yourself what you need to hear. tell yourself nothing at all. but you will get through get through. pull through. give yourself time. thinking of you.

gentle and deep.

you are gentle with kisses as you are deep with your words. i wish the world could experience your softness. your clutch. your love. the way it melts and warms and fills.

memories.

the best kind of memories are those that can never be forgotten.
no matter how hard you try to wipe them away or close your eyes
tightly they play right in front of you. as if it were yesterday. the
memories flash and flood like a puddle with no footprint. clear.
unmarked. as if when called upon the memory itself knows what
you need to hear and see and smell before the heart beats it to
play itself. my favorite memory of you rests just underneath your
rib. where our favorite word permanently lives. as skin bares
itself there it is written. it is written. it is written. right to left.
outstreched like a gravestone dripped in earth. dipped in honey.
swimming on flesh just above bone. you are the culmination of
what they say you shouldn't be. that is how i see you. framed in
no one's box. no one can ever say you aren't part of their memory
bank. see you. you are memories. ones that wake you in cold night
sweats to remind you that above your ribbed cage you have breath
and air and stars and destiny to go after. you. see. you. are loud
silence. the break between breaks in a break where it breaks.
only you would understand. you represent all the things that
disrupt lulls in days and instill a hush that catches fire and quiets
crowds. you are the short term and the forever. a new wave after
another one passes. a new moon after 29.53 days since the last
new moon. and there. right there. right. there. i see you. just
between my dreams and my awakenings. resting. resting. resting.
teasing me of our last time. our last memory. our last. our last.
until we make another last.

feel your own waters.

i looked into your eyes and finally saw you:
a well full of water not wanting to be saved
but to be understood.

eyes are truly the window into the soul. and i get why you
sometimes don't want to let someone look at you. it gives them
access to a part of you that may not want them to see. it's your
right to protect your heart. your soul. protect your mind. protect
your body. protect your energy. protect your you. you are your
own gatekeeper. and your eyes are a sacred part of you. and as you
pull from your own well to see yourself)it is about seeing you(
you are the freeing. you are the pulling. you are the gathering. you
are the filling. you save yourself every time you reach into you.
when you grant your own flow to flow and feel your own waters.

do what is right for you.

those who tell you to not hide and be yourself
are the same ones who find it difficult to live those words.
aspirational for everyone. a journeying for every soul.
do what is right for you. decide what is true for you.
take whatever words someone sentences your way
and decipher or reject or jumble and lodge
whatever needs lodging at your choosing.
at your uncovering. no one is you.
but when you finally find you.
but when you finally. find. you.
every hushed word your heart
beats will make sense.

beware.

watch those who
fill you up
just to feel you down.

ssb.

when you speak positively about yourself
you feel lighter you walk taller you exude energy
slowly.
steadily.
beautifully.

want yourself.

i want you more
the more
you want yourself.

everyone everyone.

i hope you rise this morning
knowing the world and everyone in it
loves you. everyone everyone.
thank you for that smile you just smiled.

home.

i held your hand last night. in my dream. but i was awake.
found myself looking into your eyes. wanting to be held. to hold.
went to you. went home.

thorn and thunder.

don't expect me
to always be roses
and sunshine. i'm half
thorn and thunder and
sometimes want to be
left alone to storm.

playlist.

i made a playlist for you. songs you grew up to.
songs you've made love to. songs you cried and
grew through.

can i send it to you. can i mix it for you.
can i put it on a compact disc and title it.
can i leave it where you'll reach for it.
can i make another and another and another.
just for you. all for you. to go back to.
to look at the scratches made from listening
to the tracks over and over and over and
look at the lines like the lines left on
oak trees to show how old how long
how strong our love has been. to
show how far you have grown
as a relic of a timeless love.

water you.

water you.
even if
the sun
droughts
your well.

only only.

you are the one. the only only. the expectation and the expected. the sure and the certain. the root and the sun. you pull and lure and hold and ease and open you open you open you open. you. oh you. aren't just anyone. not one other soul)no matter how hard they try(can deep like you. empath like you. gift like you. gorgeous like you. humble like you. create like you. love like you. attract like you. heal like you. energy like you. you are the one. the only only one.

terrifying and wonderful.

being in your presence is terrifying and wonderful. i wonder if you miss me when i am away. if you see me with your eyes closed or if i am lost to your memories.

don't ask persmission to be yourself.

you don't ask permission to be yourself. you just are. and in your rise in your phoenix in your blooming you ignite in others the audacity to be themselves.

three things about you, dear giver.

expect nothing in return.
people overlook what you do.
your impact may never be known.

giving is a gift. you are a gift.
sadly sadly most take advantage.
they do not see the out of your way
they only feel the ease of their breathing
not knowing it is your air that grounds them.
you are a golden giver. you are to be treasured.

bring all of you out more.

everything about you is favored. highly. even that part of you you try so hard to cover and hide. the tune of you pierces the soul. bring all of you out more.

fiery rain.

you are that fierce monsoon. that fiery rain. that force that flame.
if they can't handle a little storm they will never survive the next
season coming. notice who really wants you. who really cares. and
who really doesn't. you'll know. you'll know. those that last are
lucky. those that leave are lost.

you are a giving love.

you are a giving love. a deepest love. a full moon. a full sun. a full star. a full planet. a full wonder. beauty isn't your nickname. beauty is your first name in all languages known and unknown. and in your give in your gift in your grace is more grace more gift more give. all of you. full of you. and whoever is granted passage. granted access. granted you better deserve you. better get you. better better you. for a you like you isn't to be undered. under loved. under cared for. under wanted. under desired. under anything. for a giving love like you is all the space between space. filling from you is the best feeling.

next level love.

when you get used to someone it doesn't mean
stop trying. it means you have moved on to the
next level. you have tapped into a deeper zone.
and when you get more and more comfortable
drop further and further into one another. into
yourself. love is about unraveling and finding
more things to fawn and admire about the one
you choose to spend every season with. be sure
to fawn and admire yourself. that glow of you
rubs off and reminds your person to explore
parts of them to appreciate. honor. and cherish.

something something.

there is something something about you that collects and gathers
and holds and lifts the weight off shoulders and says with me you
have nothing to bring that will ever make me want to turn away.
you are the sigh before the sigh. a refreshing gulf of love your
person retreats to. what a treat you are. what a treat you are.

stretch with you.

i don't want to be comfortable with you. i want to stretch with you. and grow with you. and maximize the deepest deep with eyes entrusting one another. to exist with you means to always drown in self and come up to find more self to admire.

brave.

brave is the breath you take with you in the face of each day. each challenge. each encounter. nothing stops you and the voices telling you you can't get silenced every time you choose to show up. on the spot exactly when their thoughts begin to diminish you they eat their words. eat their judgments. they fall out of their shallow and go elsewhere. simply because of your brave. your fierce. your nerve to face rather than away. but in your face it doesn't mean you lack fear or lack anxiety you take those along. you bend them to your will and say if you are to come then keep quiet do not stop me. for you cannot be stopped. it is that beast in you. that rare in you. that agency in you. that valor in you. that energy in you. that rises and rises and rises and follows good winds. good vibes. good love. good good. take this line and slow down. right now. slow. slow. honor that brave in you. the b.r.a.v.e. you. the good good you. the beautiful you that deserves to be reminded even if you already know. the beautiful you that earns the right to be seen and acknowledged even if you reject it. your brave must be praised. not in reward but in regard. deep deep regard.

before your time.

stand up for what you believe in no matter if your voice trembles or your stomach is in knots. be what strength is made of. courage. vulnerability. mixed with water. people like this are before their time. you are before your time. not that you should be replicated but you should be modeled. mused. blueprinted. skeletoned. to see how you are made. what you are made of. how you courage the way you do. this world needs needs needs more and more and more of you because with you this place hits different. feels different. is different. in the best way. the only way. the way those who get you get you. one day you won't be outlier. but maybe you will always be outside. in the margin. the one holding. the one teaching. the one waying. looking to you. looking for you. thank you.

the bay.

you are unstoppable. many will try to keep you at bay but you are the bay. all the oceans. they are just streams desperate to find your source.

medal of honor.

you. in the face of unbearable. in the wake of chaos. are bold by just continuing despite the assaults. despite the tears. despite the horrors. you deserve a medal of honor.

you are a lighthouse helping guide souls home.

that you in you deserves more air. more light. more water. more fire. more more. and in the break of you is a grace of you that is always looking out for someone else when you should be pausing for you. but that is just you. trying to make someone else feel ease even if you tire and collapse from long days. helping someone else makes it worth it even if thank you never leaves their lips. you are the definition of a friend who never seeks any shine of light. shine this light on you. thankful for some you.

i look up to you. up close. from afar. quietly
yet with proud proud humility. you're doing
what you said you always wanted to do and
i see you. i see you. even if you don't think
i'm looking. i am watching through the window
you are opening for us. for those that come
after us. you are steady becoming who you
are supposed to become. and if no one ever told
you the profound magnitude your gravity means
in this lifetime let me remind you that you are
a necessary beam. a motivation that lifts others
when they want to stop climbing. that passion
in you that purpose in you that gold in you
is a lighthouse helping guide souls home.

much magic.

you are much. much magic. much needed. much love. much soul.
even you need to slow wind. to slow down. so you have enough
beautiful energy to light up the sky.

the star of stars.

mirrors were made because the muse of you.
the nature of you. the beauty of you. someone
tried to create art out of art and all they could
do was share your reflection. your flattery. your
mastery. and although you don't like to look or
draw attention to or care to know you are the
model. the exemplar. the star of stars. even
your wandering is studied. is emulated. is
marveled. because you are a marvel.
a beautiful beautiful astonishing marvel.

you more often.

you look good on you. so keep choosing yourself more often.
listen to yourself more often. trust yourself more often. be no one
else but you. you are always your best choice. look to you because
everyone else is taken.

someone's someone.

you. quiet storm. you. big heart. you. giving soul. are someone's
smile. someone's happy thought. someone's guess who i saw today.
someone's always wish. i hope you know that.

more proof.

you are proof that miracles exist. anything from you is potion. a pollutant everyone wants in their air. what oxygen you are. what oxygen you are.

you did it again.

you did it again. overgave. overstretched.
overextended. hoping this time it would be
different. hoping this time the outcome would
feel better but you just got more of the same.
more of the nothing. no matter how hard
no matter your effort no matter what you do
you can't change them. you can't change
anyone. but that doesn't mean stop being you.
it just means stop bending and breaking and
efforting for people who won't do the same
for you. take your love elsewhere. always give.
but only give to a point. protect the house of you.

their misfortune. not yours.

there are some who still believe that whoever
loves less holds the most power. and whoever
gives the least controls the relationship. this is
why things end. this is why opening up hurts.
this is why trauma exists. when people withhold.
when people play games. when people don't care.
when people don't think about how they destroy
others who just want to love and be loved.
but this is their loss and their own defeat and
their own demise when they resist being completed
by you. embraced by you. this is their misfortune.
not yours. love more on people who deserve you.

water like you.

it's been too long since you may have heard this.
may have felt this. brought it close enough to fill
up. so here it is for you to remind you. of all the
you you've been wanting someone to recognize
but they seem to always fall short)you deserve
a full tank of love not anything less(. you are
a river that runs through mountains and cuts
through lands and collects and collects and
collects all the goodness all the honey all the
beautiful life that makes you you. filling others.
spreading light. and just like rivers you run wild.
water like you is never meant to be contained.

break and begin again.

even steady waves eventually crash. you can't always expect yourself to hold it together. even your tide reminds you that you too can break and begin again.

new wings.

you've always been able to fly. high. high. so high. someone at some point got intimidated and tried to replicate your wings. they clipped yours thinking they could fly as high too but didn't have a soul like yours. and your wings just grew back stronger and you flew even higher. higher. higher. and even in their thinking they were clipping you they were just assisting you helping you shed old feathers old weight old heaviness old matters that kept you from higher heights heigher elevations higher inclines that you were always bound for but your last pair weren't enough to get you there. and whether you sheared them yourself or someone else did the shearing you already blasted off. already set towards horizon. already jetted as if gravity never existed. not discounting reality and being unable to direct traffic that comes your way or slows you down or hardens your efforts but there is always a better a goodness a lesson in the alley in the gutter in the mud in the distress that will flight you before take off is expected. new wings grow more powerful. new wings satellite you. new wings dare you. to beyond where you have already been. to challenge what hasn't been challenged. to explore what hasn't been explored. and when the time comes before you know it you soar without trying. you soar as if you have been conditioning all your life. for that chapter to turn the pages before must be written. and you've been writing with wings that don't even exist yet. but they will. and each time you cloud and turn into rain there is a rainbow you have already manifested. so keep charting your course.

infinity out of infinity.

even when you walk away and come back
you are missed. it seems you always leave
a scent of you that has all the amounts of
you to keep you still there. still memoried.
still picturesque. every highlight of you is
a ten out of ten. in person you are infinity
out of infinity. above enough. and when
people tell the story of you somehow your
smile becomes their smile. they glow like
you. you are a beautiful everlasting love.

don't remove any of your magic from you.

your smile)that smile(is its own firework show. the magic of it bursts and those near and far are you struck. awe struck. and instantly become changed. their mood if sad is reversed. their mood if happy is intensified. if stuck they are able to now move. because you move. you encourage. you be. and that is something no one can ever take away. don't take that away from you. don't remove any of your magic from you.

always be who you are.

don't change and change and change and change and forget who you are. be and be and be and be and you'll always be who you are.

turn yourself up.

you are all the sounds all at once. the most epic anthology of love there is. but you keep turning your music down low. you keep shying away from your higher calling. what we see and what we hear from you is already mesmerizing. imagine when you turn yourself up a notch and the flowetry of you commences. there will be no stopping you. you are the notes every musician composes to. just listen for yourself. hear your own sound dear muse.

the giver in you is all heart and hope.

the giver in you is all heart and hope.
this is why you are full and inspiring.

rumble.

pressure creates diamonds. and you have always
been one. no matter your circumstance. no matter
the darkness. no matter the weight. no matter the
challenge. you shine and get through and pierce
in such a way that whatever is around you feels
your rumble. feels your shimmer. needs your
light. to see how that no matter what there is a
how. there is a way. there is a chance to come
out on any side better than better. remember you
are fire in fire. diamonds in diamonds. shine on.

the antidote to feeling whole again.

your energy is the chemistry that fills empty hearts.
one glimpse of you is the antidote to feeling whole again.

in the beginning.

staring at you is like witnessing the world
being created and re-created over and over again.

when you discover yourself.

when you discover yourself you'll never
choose to be anyone else ever again.

do something brave.

explaining yourself won't do. not anymore. squeezing yourself into four corners goes against who you are and what you are all about. but like a good and thoughtful person you bend when no one else bends. you accommodate to make others happy. this is not a terrible thing. it is a skill. and. it is time to lead with your heart. to listen to that heart of you. to foot down when people do what you know in your heart is not good or kind or considerate. this is your now. to dig. to ground yourself to other possibilities of living. to not complicit when you can do something brave. because you are something brave. made of bravery. made of good. made of love. when you do that thing. that brave thing. that hard thing. that good thing. the world heals better. the world shockwaves and responds. the world slows its rotation and spotlights you. not to praise you or make you the center. but to breathe with you. to concentrate the same way you concentrate those around you. those doused in your goodness. it isn't coincidence the words good and brave keep showing up on this page as your hands as your mind as your heart absorbs these words. when you deep into your you. when you see you you sometimes have to look away because the reflection is bright)always bright(because magic can't see itself. that looking away that closing of the eyes that putting of the hands to block out the sun is what others do to you at first look at you but they can't keep their eyes off of you when you stay in your light. when you stand in your magic. when you stand in your power. not that you are unmoving or uncompromising)you overcompromise and overmove(but this is your time your harvest your obligation to unleash your wonder in this world. to unwaver and not apologize for unwavering. ahead. ahead. ahead. ahead. that confident vibe. that sticking to your truth. will be uncomfortable for those unstrong to headwinds. difficult for those unwilling to really see you. all good. still be you. still be you.

this is the time.

this is the time. your time. this time. to.
to gather. to bring. to inner. to clear. to.
let your heart sing louder. let yourself self.
to peace who needs peace and forgive you.
for holding chaos inside you for a time too
long. for a tick too strong. for someone who
should no longer have access to your energy.
for someplace that underestimates your light.
for something that pushes you away. to go.
in presence or in mind but for sure in ache.
as that time has expired to give any more
of you to what doesn't give to you.
and that sounds harsh to those who
don't know your behind the scenes.
who don't know what it means to give.
only takers see this as selfish. and those
are the ones who are out of time.
those are the ones not even on notice.
those are the ones to forget and remove.
this time. this. time.
without warning.
how you do this. how you do this. like this.
decide. trust in that decision. allow the discomfort
of it and don't let up or let in. give your mind your heart
your attention on something else that fills you. allow patience.
expect resistance. stay steady. stay the course. daily gets easier.
eventually in the rear window. in the background. in the fade.
the moving on to what is better will be worth the releasing.
but you have to release. only you know what needs releasing.
when you watch for what you become you'll bloom better love.

you are a lifetime of romance.

the very thought of you
)that thought right there(
shoots chills down backs
and rattles rattles rattles
old definitions of what
love could be ought to be
simply by being deeper
)so much deeper(simply
by being you. you are
a lifetime of romance
a spacious heart put here
to be my forever love.

your temper is wild like it should be.

there is no one way to be. there are some days you feel colorful
and expressive and playful and do so many vibrant things to
match the inside vibes to your outside life. and then there are
moments you feel cold or neutral or indecisive or reserved or chill
and you are less interested in animation and more in need to keep
you to you. to gray scale. to fade back and mute the outside world.
complex is you. moody is too often used as negative weather. but
you are human and your forecast is sometimes unpredictable.
whether you rain or shine you are still beautiful.
your temple is wild like it should be.

alluring alluring.

your love is a practice. a routine. a heartlist. a first thing in the morning sigh and the last eyes anyone would want to watch set and rise. how alluring you are. oh how alluring you are.

you are the reason. II

can't you see. can't you feel your power. that power. right there. right there. don't lose sight of your reason. your you. your every every. every part. every essence. every crevice. every sound. every motion. be the reason you look to. be the reason you were made for. turn back to page one of giver. the second installment. the second reminder before this one. the second one after the first. and on that page)the very first dedication(says what i am telling you now. that *you are the reason. but when was the last time you knew this.* remember. so here i am again. to show you again)you don't need me to show you(but i am going to. i have to. because going on as you have been going on it can feel like you have been spinning and not moving. spinning and just staying in place. going unnoticed. but i notice. i see the energy being put in and the output taken as if it should have been easy or taken less time or perceived as no big deal. anything from you is big. is essential. is the reason where you are is how great as it is. if they won't say it i will belt it. loud it. and not care who feels ousted for being late to your incredible announcement. your presence. your effervescence. if you need to walk away or put this down or bookmark this or skip this because you have heard this then do so. but not until after you hear me out one last time. being someone's reason can feel exhausting or no big deal or cause you not to believe it. but it is real. that the reason anything gets done as it gets done the way no one else gets it done is extremely beautiful and laborsome when it comes without thanks or appreciation. this whole series is for you. because of you. soak it in. soak you in. a third of the way to go and i have more for you. all for you. take a breath and turn to the next affirmation. for more reasons. more reminders. more tributes. the greatest gift to a waterfall is a mirror. so. dear waterfall. keep flowing. keep watering. keep falling. keep pouring. keep spilling. keep giving. xo.waterfall. xo.

magic like that.

you are a love supreme. the kind that turns heads and unbreaks hearts. anything from you is a wonder because from others it's impossible to give like that. to care like that. to heal like that. but you are magic like that. your love is all that. the best that. no other way to describe that but to call it supreme.

rise.

you. your own champion. you. your own love. you. your own universe. people will try to bring you down. don't waste your energy trying to stop them. let them exhaust themselves. and rise from their own dust that gets in their way.

a lifetime supply of love.

one word from you. one hint from you. is a lifetime supply of love.
all of you. all of you. is what i always want to be around.

close and deep.

you didn't know you until you let go of their idea of you. and what a human you are. what a soul you are. and no matter how long it took for you to aware or realize you were trying to meet or exceed a version of yourself through the lens of someone else you took the mirror eventually upon yourself to lens yourself to examine yourself to posture yourself and gave yourself a talking to a loving to a wondering to that wondered what it was who it was why it was if it was the you you wanted to be. the you you need to be. the you you pictured you'd become. you are a living insider that has the beautiful ability to see what others cannot because you dare to look close and deep without judgment. close and deep without retribution. close and deep without harmful motive. you close and deep to better. to water. to ground. to understand. and it is such understanding and grounding and watering and bettering that heals. and all it took)all it takes(is the letting go of ideas that don't belong to you. letting go of versions created without your deciding. letting go of one-side energies. letting go of and finding what was yours to hold onto. keep holding onto.

endless endless.

i re-read you. like my favorite poem. re-play you
like my favorite song. over and over and over again.
once of you. never enough. twice of you better than
the first. in circles. i want to go. with you. because
wherever you are i am. when we leave we find
ourselves coming back. like magnets. electric
is our love. our way. our commitment. our home.
this is us. not for anyone else to understand or be.
it is our waves that makes us us. the way we crash.
the way we tide. the way we bubble and shallow
and deep deep deep. there is no bottom. we've
never touched down. we are an endless endless love.

you are endless breath. the space between everything. you aren't selective. those that try just can't reach the depth of you. there is a free in you. there is a wild in you. there is a dream in you. there is a fire in you. and anyone determined to tame or cage or hinder any of that in you doesn't get you. doesn't deserve you. doesn't see how they should actually be inspired by rather than intimidated by. what makes you you keeps you you. and just like the last page and the pages before that this is a post-it note to note you to raise you to light you to always follow you. always keep you. always hold you. always remind you. of that incredible breath of you. of that incredible breath in you. of that wild mixed with magic mixed with wonder mixed with warrior mixed with human mixed with all the other stuff that blooms and is yet to bloom. tho endless you are you seem to always know when to return to where you came to remain humble. as if daily you come back for air to the breath of you and breathe in breathe in breathe in where you have been where you are in appreciation and gratitude for the shoulders on which you stand.

the love of your own life.

when you are the love of your own life
everything around you just feels different.

sweet breath.

so many are fascinated by you. by your appearance.
how you peer into whatever comes and remain you
remain graceful remain steady remain strong. yes
there is that beauty yes there is the attraction but
that is just a tiny fragment of the fascination. that is
only tip only icing only outside. what many latch
onto as you. but it is your roots that hold me down.
that intrigue. that animate. that ground. under what
can't be seen only felt only experienced only loved.
you only show parts of you parts of your bloom
parts of your soul for the world to see and wonder.
so much under you. in you. what a mystery you are.

the mystery of you isn't to be solved. it is to be protected. not to
be taken. but to be preserved. and knowing there is so much more
you keep to you away from many)not because you have anything
to hide but because you have every right to keep you to your self(is
the fascination. is the imagination that only those you choose get to
prove against their hypothesis of you. their wondering of you. their
appreciation of you. and whether you unfold totally or slow by slow
it doesn't matter. you are worth the wait worth the time worth the
maze to not get to the end to but get to turn by turn explore every
pathway of you in hopes never to get to the exit because leaving
you isn't the objective. loving you is the objective. time doesn't exist
around you. everything might zoom by or fly by or get used up but
there is no using you. there is only amazing you. journeying with
you. this doesn't mean your way or no way. it means the interest is
mutual. the presence is mutual. nothing one-sided about your love.
when you breathe out they breathe you in. and vice versa. breathing
you in can't be replicated without exhaling too quickly. sweet breath
you are love. sweet sweet breath you are love.

to whom it may concern.

may whoever has your love really know the jewel you are.
may whoever gets a glance at you know the wonder of a true
beautiful soul. may whoever has your attention understand
what it feels like to hold their heart in their hands.
may whoever who is granted behind the scenes of you know
you just don't open up to anyone. know it is a big deal. know
your give your grace your garden is special made treasure made
gold that never needs polishing no matter what tries to damage it.
may whoever loves you love the total you the undeniable you.
may whoever gets to spend time with you always adore you.

real and beautiful.

everyone can't see you. even if staring right at you.
some just can't see someone real and beautiful.

you are a wishing well.

you are a wishing well. whatever you wish comes true.

what good love is.

you are the standard measure
of what good love is. givers like
you don't even know it.

your aura is of stuff unfound.

your aura is of stuff unfound.
nothing about you has been discovered yet.

even if you tried you can't be compared.
not because you are above or better but
because it is impossible. you are you
and no one else can say that.
there is always something new
there is always something interesting
about you that has no adjective no
language no box to place it in. not
because you try to be out of this world
you are out of this world. it would take
planet after planet to get to a root of you.
so as you keep being the being you are
your aura glistens and intensifies
the desire to get close to you
the desire to get near you
the desire to deep with you
to only find speechless enounters
under your incredible surface.

they do not understand your magic.

when they
tell you you're
seeing things
hearing things
feeling things
they do not
understand
your power.
they do not
understand
your magic.
they aren't
supposed to.
and they
never
will.

contagious.

you have this contagious optimism.
never give that up. never give you up.

cool runnings.

the journey with you is better with one without you.

.

already yours.

you always find a way because you are the way. any way. all the ways. nothing can stop you from what is already yours.

same you. different version.

same you. different version.
but this one. this season. this
form of you. turns heads. and
yet they haven't even seen the
best parts. the finest places. the
hottest spots. not just anyone has
access to. and just when they think
they have you figured out you move
onto and into another iteration of you.
someone so multidimensional doesn't
sit still or stay idle or remain what was.
you constantly bloom into beautiful you.

you're always there. here. now.

the charm about you. the delight about you.
the marvel about you. is that you rarely share.
you give snapshots. quick mysterious highlight
reels every so often to leave breadcrumbs. leave
traces. leave scents. to fill the senses to recall
you when you are needed)you are always needed(.
you are the quiet anthem and the cause. a fault
line with no faults just beauty marks that needs
just one subtle movement and you move you move
you move even those furthest from you. stranger
to no one. a peace of home. like you weren't there.
but you're always there. here. now. now. now. now.

you are a bloom blooming blessings.

forever is a long time but a time stamped forever with you is a
life that started long before meeting you long before choice was
a choice. this. you. is a kind of magic never witnessed before. a
kind of hope never hoped before. a sight never seen before. and if
people were to blink too fast as they often do they would miss the
secret of you. the glare of you. the rare of you. not because they
don't want to but because they don't know a bloom blooming in
front of them. but you do. you are a bloom blooming blessings.

the true gem that you are.

you always belong. but this generation
doesn't know the true gem that you are.

making people feel.

your super power is making people feel
like they are the only only. no one else can
do that. thank you for doing that.

wear love like sunlight.

you may want to give up on many things.
many people. many many that feel like
pulls and wastes and tugs on your energy.
but before the last straw seek one last lesson
to see if there is anything else that can be
done. because once you are finished your
attention your all is onto what deserves you.

walk around like you know who you are
)you know who you are(and if anyone
tries to define you tell you call you by
a name that isn't yours keep walking.
keep stunting. keep stunning. keep
standing in your own determination.
in your own essence without offense.
without explanation. without fire in your
response)if you even respond(they don't
know. they don't know. they never have
seen flames under water. never seen magic
like you. you don't need their validation.

can't look away from you.
you wear love like sunlight.

and that kind of awe is a sacred moment.
a memory one deep breath away. you can't
escape your light. who would want to.

take your heart with you.

the pounding. the aching. the waiting. the shaking.
the wanting. the wanting. the wanting. the wanting.

their misunderstanding of you isn't reflection of you. you are the
oldest language unspoken. if they were really interested really
intrigued really imbued with you they would stay up study up
practice the pronunciation of you. to know as much of you as you
reveal. one thing they must know is that you are not ordinary.
not like someone they have ever met. one encounter and they are
framed by you. tranced by you. learning you they better love and
understand themselves. but this is why many don't last. missing
you is an unbearable void. unfair to have to fill that deep hole.
the mmm of you. the oof of you. the sigh of you. the ahh of you.
the ooh of you. the sounds of you. music. soulful music. moving
harmonies. moving heartbeats. upping the significance. the stakes.
the importance of loving you completely. ally. all in. paining you is
hurting you and that is a note a word a movement that shouldn't
exist in your vocabulary. but facing you is the best face to face. the
best embrace. the best coming home to. nothing is better without
you. everything you bring everything you say everything you do
is craved. is wanted. is preferred. a healing)you are a healing(a
greeting. a humming. the one most requested. the one most
grounded. you are the future of what real love is missing. wherever
you go there you are. equipped with what you need because you
are what you need. please don't forget your heart. please take your
heart with you. please take your heart with you. this place doesn't
deserve a soul like yours. but while we have you)thankful to have
you(do not surrender your heart for less than you.

always always gold.

there is so much greatness in you. and you haven't even shown what is under your mountain. imagine that. when you do that. when you dig that. how much more gold you'll strike. how much more you you'll find because when you looked before others convinced you that it wasn't gold)but it was it was always always gold(do you see it now. can you see it now. the glistening. the shining. the diamonding in the rocking in the core there is a place in you so priceless. so priceless. and even when you come across it you won't believe it. astonished you'll be. at the reflection. at the seeing. at the experiencing of self as if the first gasp of breath. pure. untainted. unbothered. the naked truth of you. stripped and clear. forget about all around and focus on just you. what do you see. what do you feel. what do you need that is already there. it is there. did you close your eyes. did you slow your speed to rush through this line to get to the next line. i'll ask again. did you close your eyes. now. where are you. where did you take you. do you feel the space around you. the ground under you. the energy between you and the you you're thinking of. that greatness there. that untapped greatness there. grab hold of it now. tightly to it now. tightly to you now. bring it up. bring it up. bring it up. clench it to your chest. are you clenching it. how does it feel. how do you feel. look down at where you are holding. open your eyes. do you see it. do you see you. how do you look. now look up. your crown is waiting for you to place it back on your head.

dear you. beautiful beautiful you.

you are here. outstreched. still here. and being here took a toll
to get here. yet. you. persevered. too many thank you's and i
appreciate you's and i see you's and i love you's and wow how
amazing you are's failed to reach you. failed to fill you how you
needed to be filled. maybe they wish those vows honored you but
for their own reasons they hostaged them. but do not hold your
breath hoping what you need from them will come. perhaps their
window is closed. and you are better off flying through your own
onto better mountaintops. you. the river. you. the source. you. the
outlet. have experienced so much in a year. so much to proclaim.
and my how you've grown. my how you've overcome. my how
you should be proud of you for the days you didn't want to get
up)but you did(be proud of you for finishing when you wanted
to quit)you didn't quit(be proud of you for the bloom you can't
even see)you've bloomed you've beautifully bloomed(. look at
you. look at you. look. at. you. all the tears have watered you into a
more incredible you. take you with you. give more and more and
more and a thousand more lives will benefit from your light. you
will benefit from your light. hold onto you. be a bit more gentle
with you. give yourself more give this year. this season. this new
opening. give you back to you when that negative inner critic rears
itself to thorn you by saying go away not today i'm fine i don't
need you. because there will be days you aren't going to take ease
on you and you'll be too harsh too pressured too coarse. that's
okay. give grace. give love. give pass. give safe harbour. do what
best serves you. outsiders will pull you in and try to convince you
and corner you and use you to fill them up and leave you drained
without a care of how they abused your heart. be prepared for
that. brace for that. and when you see it before it happens protect
yourself. it's your right to defend your castle.

stand in your fire.

your shrine. nothing selfish about preventing the same patterns from getting near you again. so much further to go but relish and admire you. stand in your fire and awe at your polish. at your essence. at your life. at your yours. look at what you have accomplished. relish and admire you.

out of your head. into your heart.

the vow you vowed needs no revowing but since you are on this note it needs revisiting. it can be a lot for you all those hours going back and forth in your mind. the vacation can't even be considered a vacation because you have been there such an extended time it is time to take a leave of absence up north and breathe down south take a train or plane or even walk to the doors of your heart and rest and beach there a time. to feel again. to feel what it is like to experience the beat instead of playing back images that happened or haven't happened but your body hasn't gotten the change to absorb it only categorize it. sigh. take another breath. one step closer away from those thoughts and into the passageway of what has been awaiting your return it may be something you haven't acknowledged and unfamiliar as to how to keep your mind out of it and let your heart into it. into you. you may believe you have forgotten but the body never forgets. breathe. breathe. breathe. give yourself permission to aware those thoughts that are buzzing trying to trespass and keep you from emotion and let them go by in peace as you renew your contract with you. breathe in you some more. what is coming up for you. if you are feeling the need to cut this stay short breathe in again and appreciate your honesty and stay a bit longer. just a bit longer. there has been vacancy in your heart for so long for so long for so long that it can be strange in your own home but when you choose to give you more of you this is what happens. what has to happen. what needs to happen. this doesn't mean stop listening to your mind completely. this means start listening to your heart morely. from this day forwardly. to give you a chance to give you a break to give you the love you have been avoiding. stay as long as you can as long as you want and when you are ready listen to what your heart has to say.

your tattoo says.

so many)so many(want to know what your tattoo says. what your
tattoo means. when did you get it. why did you get it. what others
do you have. and that is reasonable. that is fair. that is their way
of being curious about you. and sometimes you get tired of
explaining of sharing of storying of guiding of opening up your
canvas. not everyone has to know. sometimes you just want to be
and let be. to flower without explaining your flowers. to grow
without explaining your growth. your tattoo says what it says.
let that be that. the ones who you want to let in on your beauty
will find the answers when the light is just right.

the change no one else can see but you.

you made the conscious decision to do what was right. and it took some time. many times before you chose had heavier reason for others heavier reason for validation heavier reason to prove to others. and that isn't bad or wrong or worse than where you are in life now. it got you to the threshhold of deciding a bit deeper. asking the harder questions getting under the under and under more without feeling the need to defend yourself. because when you do it for you there is nothing to defend. you became a grander lifestyle of the life you once lived because filling you better was the best option because at the end of each day you report to you. you look you in the mirror with one question. *was i true to you.* may sound simplistic or basic but sometimes basic and simple gets us out of our own way to cut through the noise into a truth we desperately try to avoid. and there is no more avoiding you. so in your maturity you know not everyone will recognize the shift recognize the work recognize the growth recognize the transformation but that doesn't matter. you are the change no one else can see but you. there is a quality that didn't exist before that fills crisper now. that fills different now. that fills better now. there is a newfound air that was always there)always there(you just had to choose to become what you always were.

joy is everything around you.

joy is everything around you. you go about looking for people and places that endlessly give you life and energy and often wonder why people always want to be around you always want to seek you always want to accompany you. it is because you are their joy. their happiness. their best to be with. hands down. no questions asked. first choice. joy. they are thinking of you now and will soon reach to you and ask you what it is you are doing hoping you will join them for some time. their time. to bring them back to equal. back to baseline. back to home.

connected to everything.

the life. the vibe. the attraction.
clearly the universe's favorite.
you are connected to everything.
a magnet of divine love.

this volume is for you love.

whatever your love is i want to be fluent in it. whatever language you speak i want to be fluent in you. whatever your sign is i want to translate it. whatever your heart wishes i want to grant it. not sure if you ever heard these words or felt these requests but they are real and true and take your time if you need to think about your response. because as you always do what it is you do you can often not see why anyone would say such things or mean such things but press those to the side and take this in. flare this in dear you. if you ever question if you're beautiful you are. if you ever doubt you're enough you are. if you ever wonder how i feel i feel everything and more for you. this ode to you is a pause for you. to come up for you. to smile for you. if you're not smiling i hope you're smiling now. for you. with you. let it come through. my goodness you look good on you. the fragrance of you is the best bloom on this earth. nature's finest doesn't even know its the finest and that is the honest truth about you love. it is not that you are above compliments love. you just don't see what the big deal about you is and that is why this volume is for you love.

the smile you wear.

the smile you wear is a candle in the dark. a light in chaos
a lifeboat always in reach. even a slight grin awakens a cold world.

the deepest refill.

you are the deepest refill. everflowing. overflowing. undercurrent.
neverending wanted most)always wanted most(. one drop of you
in the system of another and they can go on for a whole century.
inside you is a reserve a specialty a brew that elixes fixes heals
fills fills fills and just gets better each time. you make better
every time. not many give you loving quality like that.
like a filling wholeness wholesome holding that
forever lasts. you are a forever lasting love.

kind. clear. good.

kind. clear. good.
you in three words.

don't wanna be known.

you don't wanna be known for anything other than love.
for anything other than compassion. for anything other
than positive. it's not as if you are looking for perfect
)there is no such thing(you just can't stay around
situations not intended for healthy blooming.

standing up for yourself.

you sometimes think that standing up for yourself puts people off so you downplay how you really feel. but standing up for yourself teaches people what you stand for and you won't be stood on.

the right piece to cherish you.

when you stop looking
for what you are looking
for it comes to you faster
quicker as if you weren't
looking in the first place.
that's because you create
space within you for
the right fit to find
you. the right
piece to
cherish
you.

meet you where you are.

becoming who you are meant to become is a slow process. an intentional process. there aren't really any answers just a lot of questions. reflections. mirrors for you to look into. it's normal to want to know if you are where you need to be and if you made the best choice the best decision the correct conclusion but that is the puzzle. to not really know. to place one heart after the other and trust. and recalibrate and come back to you at the next junction. to meet you where you are and appreciate where you've been.

every breath they breathe.

someone has been waiting for you.
songing for you. talking about you.
even now. even now. you are the
longest bridge that crosses their
heart. and they can't stop. you
are imprinted and etched on
every breath they breathe.
there is no escaping you.
no one would want to.
they see you as you
should be seen.
beautifully.

hold on to that smile you give to others.

you make everything feel better. it might be because of the tones you use. or maybe the approach you take. or maybe there is what can't be named that you do. whatever it is you are a marvel. even as days get longer and you can't hold on to that smile you give to others and you need to retreat into a corner and blanket yourself under what helps you forget your own pain your own aches your own struggles your own reservations there is light)your light(that flutters and pulses and hovers and covers what is sharp and like the alchemist you are turns bitter moments into better into better into better days are coming even as days get longer and you can't hold on to that smile you give to others hold on to that smile hold on.

hold you like you hold the world.

someone
wants to
catch you
hold you
like you
hold the
world
softly
gently
lovingly
strongly
lightly.

what dawn feels like.

there is a secret ingredient nestled close)real close(lodged somewhere neath your skin tween your soul and ribcage. meet me there. treat me there. that is where what dawn feels like. warm and unknowing. a blessing to see with eyes wide. an honor to love the sun. a treasure to wake up next to. you)secret ingredient(are every matter that matters. every hope that hopes. every shine that shines.

you deserve to be flooded back.

you normalize giving. to a degree that must be broadcast. the fact that you give unto others as you would want given to you and fully mean it fully emit that is a whole loving language in and of itself. some just talk aspirationally about wanting to show up but excuses flood their lungs. some walk without talking and that is you. all you. just doing. showing. being. caring. giving. spreading light spreading love spreading authenticity even when it never floods back. you deserve to be flooded back.

beyond the 1:1.

some create a fantasy world. a realm that is just pixels and countdown smiles. filters and color schemes. nothing real and rare there except the character of make believe. the screen becomes just an extension of who they want you to see. a tiny percentage of happily just in that moment hoping to get quick doses of dopamine. but you are beyond the 1:1. beyond the box. beyond the confines. you share some things. you share no things. you keep it one hundred and not what is expected to get validated. there is nothing false or empty or half or hollow about you. what you see is what you get. and of you so much is offered. too much for many. everything for the right. for the deserving. for the true. if love were a ratio you'd always be full. always the greatest. always the proof. that going off a social grid instead of staying inside one is of benefit. is of accolade. because in person you are way more than what a decompressed image allows.

a question that no one has ever asked you.

a question that no one has ever asked you gets asked.
the one you have waited for and waited on and prayed for just
knows it has never been articulated your way before)not this way
before. not this how before(. and it drops your heart into another
realm you thought only you would occupy. that you would be
alone in. not because you are lonely)your solitude rejuvenates
you(but because you are particular about the kind of energy that
swarms around you. so when they say it and it leaves their person
it doesn't leave their lips it souls out of them and souls into you.
unlocking a response you have been wanting to respond to
without words simply by heart. the beating to find the beat
and it be harmonious and blends into you without dissonance
without strain without you doubting its entrance. this question
)that question(more like a clause. a clause that simply states
a joining that was already written that was already envisioned
that was already there a meeting place just hadn't been
established yet and in the fine print an ellipsis
with nothing in front or at its end. a just.
a waiting. a bridge. for you to fill in.
for you to continue and write
your own.

you are life changing.

to be seen by you is life changing.
you are life changing.

how to see. how to look. how to between the lines.
the viewing)your viewing(is unmistakable. undeniable.
remarkable. can't believe it took me so long to see. i was looking
but wasn't seeing. what a seeing you are. everything missing was
here all along. you all along.

oof.

oof is the sound the heart makes
when you come around.

what i want to tell you.

i love you.
that's what
i want to
tell you.
all day.
always.
every
every
every
every.
you are
my heart.
you are
my soul.
you are
words
never
said.

your love.

your love is unquestionable. uncapturable.
uncaptionable. unanything and all things wow.
all things awe. all things magnet that gravitate
that attract that pull that covers that heals you
are a beautiful healing. a beautiful sounding.
a beautiful coming. you are a collection
of nature's beauty mixed with god and
universe and honey and gold. your
love is describable only in waves
and vibrations and vibes and
it is worth mentioning here
you have the best heart.

your magic.

not sure how you do it. but you do it. you turn sadness into
sunshine. but not before you allow yourself to feel what needs
to be felt. not before you allow yourself to sit with all of you that
needs more attention than the rest. and then you turn everything
into light. into love. into holy love. just thought you should know
that i notice your magic love. i notice you're magic.

mind your pour.

that temporary fix
will still itch if you
keep pouring
expectations
into a relationship
that isn't mutual.

this doesn't need a title.

you are everything you need. today.
you have everything you need. today.

no need to question yourself. today.
no need to define yourself. today.

gift to the world.

you've been waited on. waited for. longed for. prayed for. needed for. even as i say this there is someone)that someone(wanting you. to have the best. to feel the best. to make this day and all days deserve you. because what you deserve is more. not because what you have isn't enough. but because it's hard to return the gift you gift the world. thank you for being a gift to the world.

full bloom.

you sometimes give in. may have given in a bit more give than you wanted to. but that is you. the amnesty of you. to naturally go above and above and above and above and above even if what you get back in return is below)way way below(. so much heir of you. so much air in you. what is coming will meet you where you are so don't stop giving you. you are in full bloom dear giver. xo dear giver.

it's okay to be sad love.

this season can get lonely. and sadness can creep up. creep in. and if it does)i know it does(i am here. standing here. waiting here. i never went from here. i never went away. those others astray those others dissappear but you know my love like your love is in the space between each gasp between each breath. it's okay to be sad love. here for rain and shine love. just wanted to let you know love.

even if the sky is falling.

even if the sky is falling i will hold whatever is left with you.

misunderstood.

sometimes you have feelings that greet you without warning and you don't know the matrix of ways to explain them. sometimes your actions have no purpose other than what was needed in the moment but the act itself relieved part of your being.

sometimes you can't explain away how you feel.
maybe you aren't supposed to.

sometimes you can't explain away an action.
maybe you aren't supposed to.

maybe you allow what is trying to come through you come through you and let it be. let it be.

maybe you aren't so misunderstood after all.
you're just trying to live. and that is understandable.

too many years doubting yourself.

you have spent too many years doubting yourself. and now)before now(it is time to be done with that. done with that practice. done with that habit. it took up too much space and deprived you of what you could have been doing what you could have been loving what you could have been appreciating but instead you were undoing you. and instead of getting down on you for that just get right with you. thank you. forgive you. for doing what you had to do to try and make sense of a world that had no answers for you. this way of soothing just delayed you. but no more delay. no more uncertainty. no more fear that keeps you in place take that fear with you to the place all that doubt kept you in place from. those stories that were reciting from other voices that became your own can now not just be muted but be deleted from your being. you did the human thing)it is normal to do the human thing(but now is the time to push back on all that human nature and re-direct that energy into trusting yourself and believing yourself and drive yourself to a better beyond. to a better you that never should have doubted you in the first place. so here you are. in that chapter or on another. if it creeps back in peace it out. doubt is helpful only in the beginning phase of things just to be told to not come around you anymore. it always finds its way. let it. but don't let it enter you and decide for you. counter you. control you. that old you has taught you so much. and now you and now you and now you has the come back to kick all that doubt to the curb.

what you know about giving.

it can't be empty.
it can't be returned.

your own you.

no one knows you like you know you. the intuition of you. the
sighs of you. the highs of you. the hopes of you. the ins of you. and
as you dedicate and re-dedicate your life in the pursuit of bettering
you there are faults you will come across and you may blame you
entirely for what happened for what happens and that is mature of
you. that is honorable of you. but it isn't all on you. you can't carry
what isn't yours to carry anymore. own your part. own your stuff.
own your truth. don't let it define you as the only piece of you.

take care.

that heart of yours yearns for what it yearns for and make no
mistake you shouldn't have to justify your yearning. you have
earned every yearn because your kind of heart deserves it.

so take care of what interests you invigorates you excites you joys
you fills you ignites you heals you loves you. you even thinking
about it gets you closer to it don't go further away from it. how you
flow towards it is inspiring all by itself. whatever you water grows.
and that kind of philosophy)your kind of philosophy(is the kind
of care you always take with you. even if you think you're on an
island doing as you do there is someone in the distance observing.
waving. wanting. waiting. to see your blueprint. to see how you do
it. to see how you do you. but to them effortless is your behind the
scenes they don't see all that work it takes just as you come up for
air. take care. of your heart. of your health. of your mind. of your
energy. you already do that. i know you already do that. but not
enough. there is still some yearning in you that hasn't been watered
lately or hardly ever so get to it. get to you. give back to you. take
care of you.

the real you is better than the idea of you.

it isn't on your shoulders to maintain a picture someone has of you in their head. it is on your shoulders to maintain the person you are day to day and be proud of who you are. you are not make believe and you aren't without moments you wish no one knew about or could see. you can't try and become a still photo or a one-time fantasy. who you are as is cannot live up to what someone else has planned for you unless you decide that is the lane you want to lay your heart on. it's when you direct you that you feel like you. when you expose yourself to the world with interest to see what is out there instead of the world forcing itself onto you you expand yourself and reflect on yourself. what is great about you is you do this quicker than most. you are an early adopter. an early trier. an early riser. ahead of the status quo. undictated. self motivated. interested in how to peel back your layers to see what the new winds feel like on your skin. but you wall up when it feels forced. when you feel like someone is telling you what to do or where to go or how to be. this resistence is your call to wild. you left the cage they tried to put you in a long time ago. if they knew you they wouldn't push you. you can't be pushed. you can't be pushed anywhere your soul can't flutter and fly and this you)this you(is the real you. the best you. not because you are anti-anyone but because you are pro-you. and pro-you knows you. you are for you. you are for anything and everything that doesn't try to contain. you give that. you breathe that. you gift that. no wonder the air people breathe in when near you is life. is liberating. is light. is love. you don't try to play up to be who you are not so others can see elevate you or see you as highly. you make space for everyone to be free. their free. their version. more of you. we need more of you.

wounds into wisdom.

wounds into wisdom doesn't mean you are healed. it means even if you are still hurting you turn hardship into lessons.

excuses.

excuses are easy to make but honesty is the clearer route. the
clearer way. the clearer obligation. so there is no room for doubt
or need to follow anything false with another false. when you
lead like this there is nothing to be held against you except your
decision to be true. and truth)your truth(is too bright to deny.

words you don't need to say.

this day this week this month this year has been trying. has been
challenging. has been something i wasn't prepared for but i needed
this time to focus on my life which has seemed to ravel and unravel
simultaneously and i couldn't divert my energy to anyone else but me
and those i am responsible for until some sort of calm calmed and i
am not sure when there will be space to unplug from this whirlwind
but that doesn't mean i don't care for you. this means i care deeply
for you so i am making sure i am good so that we are good. it may
seem like i have been absent but i have been here. always here.
never question my here for you. prioritizing me right now which is
necessary right now. cheering for you even if you don't hear from me
like you used to. i know you are doing what you have always been
doing and continuing to bloom and grow and do what you set out
to do. if you have wondered where i went as if i dropped off or you
did something wrong or offended me you made no offense or did
anything. i'm the last person you should think that about. we're too
close for that to be the case. i'm just choosing me. i'm just choosing
me. for a little bit longer. for a little. bit. longer. our connection
matters so i know you understand this. hearting you from afar.

the magnitude of you. the magic of you.

the magnitude of you. the magic of you. such an incredible lightness that comes from your person. in your possession there is an unknown essence that doesn't need naming because there is no name for it it's just you. it's just you. how you. close my eyes think of all you do. missing you occurs even as these words are inhaled by you just knowing you exist is all the blessings i need to get me through to the next second i just thought of you. again. how i usually do. but you don't know my entire everything craves you. to be next to you. to rub off some of you to take with me to make sense of being away from you. the magnitude of you. the magic of you. needed you to know that your gravity is the only only that keeps me still.

how enough feels.

imagine you. in all of your all. covered in your every every.
being you being you. that's how enough feels.

the sky they couldn't see.

when you wonder why enough times it can sometimes always
denominator to you. as if it was because of you. blame falling onto
you. and that's what you have been accustomed to. absorbing the
blows adjusting to make the others have to adapt less because you
think you can just change the world one you at a time. and that is
that big heart of you. your heart reacts naturally to self destruct
first before any construction happens in others. but this common
denominator has a new equation that boils down to something
you are last to say because it is too selfish. too unhumble. too out
of your vocabulary but the new practice is in finding new words
that protect you better. the new ritual is in being a bit more fire
and rock to protect you better. the new devotional is in being
more boundary and outspoken to protect you better. anytime
someone passes you by passes you up forgets you're a priority
it is because you are the sky they couldn't see. the sky they can't
see. the height they can't reach. flex that phrase a bit more today.
sharpie it on your skin so it stains a bit longer. the sky they
couldn't see. the sky they couldn't see. the sky they couldn't see.
the sky they couldn't see. the sky they couldn't see. the sky they
couldn't see. the sky they can't see. the sky they can't see. the sky
they can't see. the sky they can't see. the sky they can't see. the sky
they can't see. the sky they can't see. the sky they can't see. the sky
they couldn't see. the sky they couldn't see. the sky they couldn't
see. the sky they couldn't see. the sky they couldn't see. the sky
they couldn't see. the sky they can't see. the sky they can't see. the
sky they can't see. the sky they can't see. the sky they can't see. the
sky they can't see. the sky they can't see. the sky they can't see. the
sky they couldn't see. the sky they can't see. the sky they couldn't
see. the sky they can't see. the sky they couldn't see. the sky they
can't see. the sky they couldn't see. the sky they can't see.

wanting to be your dreams.

you can hang all the stars in your window all you want
and think they are there to help you see at night. they
are there nearest you wanting to be your dreams
wanting to be your light. wanting to be your
adornment to shine brighter and report
back to the universe letting it know
you're good. you're good.

signet.

the scar across your heart is a badge your person
wears as their signet as their sign as their banner
to never hurt you. to protect you. to love you.
until forever comes. until always rises. until
the end of time. they know you don't need
protecting)you can protect yourself(but
there is deep honor in giving what you
give in return. you deserve that love.

hearing you is the greatest hearing.

hearing you is the greatest hearing. even if no words come out you are heard loud and clear. soft and pure. nothing from you is palpable energy. the way you connect with space and the space of others and blend the space and settle settle settle any tension any worry any exclusion any insecurity any sorrow and make it feel like home. like belonging. like relief. oh relief. deep relief. you don't cure sadness but you allow sadness to join and my what a difference that makes. what a difference you make. where you are so many are willing to go just to get close to your healing. close to your filling. close to your loving. five minutes with you is a hint of beautiful infinity and each thing you say or do not say lingers in hearts and minds. they can feel you now. listening to you now. envisioning you now. calling you now. approaching you now. hearing you is the greatest hearing. even if no words come out you are heard loud and clear. soft and pure.

fluid fluid.

there is no box you fit in. no category to break you down to the smallest parts or define your identity. you are a fluid being. a fluid fluid being. being one way one day and another way the next and another in-between whatever feels comfortably you. you flow. you here and there. you to and fro. how dare anyone try to label you love. no label comes close to name you.

lost a'int lost.

wandering as you wander
is a purposeful position
you embed regularly.

direction to a spirit such as yours
depends on where your wind blows
within.

this quest)your quest(
is not to be understood
or explained.

lost a'int lost
you're finding
your finding.

no filter.

you.

there is no need to cover your light love.

half and half.

water.
whiskey.
honey.
wild.

you are mixed with horizon and the troposphere where weather is mastered. the sun stays on so not to miss the crash of your sand when the moon attempts to pull you in. the power)all that power(and all you do is be. all you do is be. water. whiskey. honey. wild. you start fires that can never be put out. you can't possibly be human. you are half cosmic half magic. a beautiful concoction.

the lucky ones.

those that know you in real life.
those that get to feel your sunlight.
those that love you for being you.
those that talk directly to your soul.
those that want you to be true.
those that respect your grind.
those that need nothing from you.
those that care about your heart.
those that see you see you see you.
those that listen to your tears.
those that enter your water.

you can't always choose where you end up but wherever you end up and whoever ends up in your surrounding are blessed to have you. some don't know a legend until someone points it out to them. others know a legend when they are standing in front of an energy field they never felt before. your vibe is on another vibe that has no language. that has no bounds. that has no comparison. those that know and don't know eventually will. but those that know know from day one day one are the lucky ones. the lucky ones. who get to view you from the best view.

nature.

all that draw from you all that draw towards you
heal better. heal quicker. heal wholly. heal fully.
that is how nature works. breathing you in
is a universal curing.

youmore.

the mantra.
the call.
the action.
the reminder.
the reason.
the responsibility.
the task.
the work.
the duty.
the affirmation.

trophy trophy.

the goal the measure the standard the award the bar the muse
you are your own tune to your own beat to your own rhythm
and there is nothing you can do about a wonder like you
except look to you as a beacon as a lighthouse as a
guide to remember that being boldly you despite
the ease of being someone else is beautiful
is brave is inspirational is necessary
even if you sometimes don't
feel like being you. you
choose you each
time.

vision.

seeing you. among all the things you have created all the goodness planted and sprouted. isn't the only justification needed to bring this to your attention to highlight your ambitions and your foresight for what you knew would happen because you manifest what comes you put out into the ether what you want and it occurs. **loving you**. for not just that big heart you have. for not just your showing up when you're drained when you have zero in your tank when you're down to your last last when you want to be left alone but you show up anyway. for not just your selflessness. for not just your giving. for not just your hearting. for everything. for everything. **wishing you**. the best life. the best love. the best joy. the best fulfillment. the best adventure. the best what's to come. you deserve the entire entire and so much more. so much more. **wanting you**. to not give up. to stay your path. to trust yourself. to want your wants. to follow your heart. to heal your wounds. to learn all the learnings. to see the world you make better. **hoping you**. treat yourself kind. give yourself grace. **reminding you**. you are a vision. you are a beautiful soul. you are the deepest breath. you are the brightest light. you are the bestest touch. you are the highly favored. take this in again. take this everywhere with you. an ode dedicated to my favorite you.

there there.

bring to me news of your day. not the roses)the roses are fine(
but mostly the thorns. i want the thorns. those that kept you
from getting out of bed. those that stressed you from being
your full self. those that tightly wound your mind you couldn't
think straight. bring me the journey and not the destination)the
destination is wonderful(but i crave your process. the scenes you
keep from surface that you keep in the depths of you. everyone
else can have the highlights. the reels. the happys. the highs. the
triumphs. the accolades. the pinnacles. but i want to be your well
and your woes. a safe space for you to bring the shadows of you.
everyone else expects just to hear the goods i want to sit with you
during the bads. during the battles. during the hard times that
keep you from trying to bloom. because there)there there(is the
you that needs air that needs light that needs love. not from me.
you have that. you don't need that there from me. what you need
is a partner to just be in your there. present in your there. patient
in your there. hand in your there. hold in your there. as you fall
into as you leap into as you crawl into as you ball into as you look
into as you heart into the water you are made of there. i'm not like
anyone else. you're not like anyone else. this is my commitment to
you. i can hold my breath and submerge with you. i want to.
take me with you. there with you. there. there.

effective immediately.

no longer give to dried up relationships.

peace.

peace. a place. a feeling. a state. a mindset. all in one. and your
dedication to uncover this peace isn't your attempt at achieving
happiness. it is your attempt to weave a sense of calm in chaos.
happiness is that mirage in a desert you reach for but it ends
up being further and further and you keep doing the same
thing to reach for it. peace is enjoying what you have
right under your feet right in your hands right in
your heart resolved that the other side isn't
going to fill your bucket. peace is a deep
internal awe that gratitude itself is
grateful for. you always know
how and where to look.

in case no one told you today.

your work is essential.
your light is essential.
your voice is essential.
your kind is essential.

how sad it is that people can go for so long without hearing affirmations. without knowing how people feel about them. without anything but being taken from. thankfully there are those like you who take it upon themselves to remind people that they are seen that they are loved that they are cherished that they are essential. but who rechargers the givers. who reignites the lightsmiths and the lightworkers and the caregivers and the rescuers who mission to supply and keep supplying even when their own supply gets depleted. you can be that one that goes on and on and on and on without the replinishment but damnit there has to be balance under the shoulders you stand. thank you for being rock and anchor and core and all the things that go unseen that go unappreciated that go unnoticed. i notice. i notice. i know. i know. you are desperately the reason there is decency and hope and love fostered in this world. i couldn't go much further without you. i can't go any futher without acknowledging you. i honor you.

i love this about you.

you are too

too wild.
too fierce.
too spirited.
too humorous.
too intelligent.
too abundant.
too magic.
too incredible.
too outstanding.
too talented.
too powerful.

to not be told this
on a daily basis

i love this about you.
xo.

caption.

a soul with wings only some can see.
a soul with lungs only some can breathe.
a soul with heart only some can love.
a soul with water only some can deep.

a smile's smile.

you are what cause smile's to smile. did you know that.
the downest down no longer can frown when sensing
you when seeing you. that is how inspiration works
that is how your love works. in decibels. in jules.
in joules. in the sighs you sigh. in the sigh
you just sighed. you can't even keep
yourself from smiling. you are
infectious beauty.

you should be here.

pause here. for a moment here. breathe here. silence here.
reflect here. be here. don't turn to the next page quite yet.
not yet. you won't know you need to do this until you
find this. and now that you stumbled across this follow this.
check your pulse here. slow your self here. no need to rush here.
take another deep breath here. okay here. you are okay here.
what you are going through needs no introduction here.
already know here. you can be here. be here. be. here.
it's not about forgetting here it is about honoring here.
it is about watering here. it is about you here)all
about you here(and in this limited time i have
with you know i have been thinking of you
a lot of thinking about you here. wishing for you here.
welling for you here. praying for you here. waiting for you here.
among words i have never said. i don't want them to go unsaid.
you should be here. every thought i have is you dear.
i miss you when you aren't here. with you there was always
always bliss. always bliss. always the right amount of what
was needed before i knew i needed it. i'm just trying
to tell you what you do to me. what you've done to me.
what you injected into my system. how do you tell the sun
you burn for it. how do you tell water you thirst for it.
how do you tell the galaxy you yearn for it. i can only return the
light and water and stardust in your direction in hopes that its
air reaches you how you reach me. this may have been my only
chance to somewhat fill an already full soul. so if you are still here
still interested still fanning these cool flames compared to your
blaze know that i adore the ground you exist on. no better way to
say that i'm not so good with words love. thank you for being here
love. come back again love. here for you always love.

seeyour.

(see'yer) **noun.** 1) someone who invests in uncovering the invisible
in people 2) someone with the keen ability to look underneath
and carry no judgments 3) someone that holds space for those
learning how to breathe on their own 4) someone willing to reveal
uncommon definitions of love 5) someone with a rare soul sharing
their story inspiring others to do the same 6) someone who
chooses to explore unexplored layers of themselves and others
with no expectation for change to occur just the creation of more
light 7) someone with a calling to practice self love 8) someone
who gives their heart to those that deserve it.

regret.

you will regret it if you don't listen to your intuition
the next time you feel an imbalance.

you change the culture.

a few more notes for you. dear giver. stay with me. dear giver.

a culture is only as good as its individual contributors. the ones
steady searching for their higher vibration their calibration their
wave to leave in the ocean when its all said and resaid when they
become ripples. what it is you have established already is being
emulated. you can't keep from being emulated. the texture of you.
the hue of you. the stride of you. no longer yours. relax the stress
that induces because that is the life of a muse. the life of a giver.
and your life should be as stress free as it possibly can be without
you grudging over pieces of you people inspire over. flakes of
you don't diminish you. you are a change agent. you change the
culture. you change cultures. and that can feel like something you
would never admit to but it's true. you say do this it is done. you
say do that it is done. you say go here it is flooded. you say go
there it is overcapacity. your pull is a power no one else has.

you change the culture. II

they can never take what you plant and have it grow the same.

you change the culture. III

change is an inside job. and from the inside out you flare into
something more beautiful than you were before. like a daily
blooming and reblooming. the good that you are the great that
you are the wonder that you are still has un untapped reservoir.
that is a sacred finding you don't have to disclose but it comes out
because it is part of you. it is part of your showing up. your light
isn't your light without pieces of that untapped staying untapped.
don't give that away. don't give that away. you provide an
overabundance already. saving you some you is how you are even
able to pour how you are able to spill how you are able to give
you to the world that doesn't comprehend the present of you the
way it should. so piece by piece when you go inside and solitude
and home and retreat and peace and peace and peace there is
no need to announce or display or share your privacy. they can't
have everything. they don't deserve everything. your everything is
yours to shelter and protect and love without gaze or distraction
or audience. your changing isn't to be witnessed until you are
ready and you never have to be ready.

you change the culture. IV

you can't change people but you can change the people you are involved with. and a change in you impacts those around you. they either appreciate it or lose contact with you. there is no in-between. not anymore. gray area isn't inhabited space any longer. too much allowance for being taken advantage of happens there. so either it is love and love or nothing at all. this is how culture shifts.

agency.

close-knit. driven. goal-oriented. unapologetically original.
hopeful. loving. kind. non-toxic. heart-centered. loyal.
diverse. inclusive. equitable. open. accessible. honest.
fun. joyful. spacious. flexible. transparent. inspiring.

the type of community you deserve to thrive around.
the type of friends you deserve to love around.
the type of relationships you deserve to be watered by.
the type of agency you deserve to have time pass by.

such heart can be found there. no need to pretend there.
no need to play up to there. just being there your entire
being there. a different kind of thriving happens where
this exists. a purity unfolds and everyone can be without
fighting for space fighting for light fighting for love
fighting for anything everyone already should have
infinity of. you know that place. you know that person.
you are that place. you are that person.

for the agency.
they know
who they
are.

finally found.

you don't know this)how would you(but i think i finally found you.
tracing and chasing your outline all this time before mustering up
the courage to dive into you just so i could bring as much proof back
to you that shows all of you that i fell into and never could look back.
no one can look back when they crash into you. are you ready. can i
report back. will you cringe at my findings or will you think i made
this up. will you prepare a response or will you just let what is said
be said and the sun rise to your grand rise. there is no one starting
point to start so let's choose your eyes)those eyes(where mystery
begins. such jewels that cut through guise and soften even the crudest
coldest souls not worth your glance. your no nonsense smirk that
says i'm kind but don't take it as weakness. i'm beautiful but don't
mistake that to top my wit and brilliance and a trillion traits that
are listed way above what it is you think you see. your soul. how it
flutters about. how it glances over your shoulder and wraps around
your waist and glides you as you walk)that soul(is the mountain
under your water. the reason words even exist to explain this. i could
go on but will instead bring up your body. the way you carry it. the
way you lift it. the way you confidence it. the way you elegant it.
the way you adorn it. you can tell you take care of the skin you are
in. how you're unafraid of its angles and armour it how you want
to armour it. but when i got to your heart i forgot about all that
other stuff. a light i've never experienced before. yes you just don't
let anyone in and there are walls but that is where i saw you. finally
saw you. finally found you. stripped of reservation and fear that isn't
allowed near you and the joy)such joy(that is where you took my
heart. that is where i lost my heart. in finding you where you let me
in. please allow me forever to stay next to you love.

ancestor love.

i more than see you. i am more than proud of you. i am more than all the things you stay up thinking worrying stewing about. no need to lose sleep thinking worrying stewing sadding longing reaching to become anything more than you already are. you are as you should be. doing beautiful meaningful exceptional things making everything and everyone brilliantly better. brilliantly deeper. brilliantly brilliant. those tears those aches those pains those thorns aren't being held against you)have never been held against you(to keep my love away from you. to keep my arms away from you. to keep my awe away from you. no one is you. thankful for you. all the pieces that you cringe about all the pieces you shy about all the pieces you shame about all the pieces you cover about all the pieces you haven't met yet there is unconditional love for. unconditioned love for. nothing you have to give up for. bring all your pieces wherever you go love. i more than see you. i am more than proud of you. i am more than all the things you think you have to be perfect and finished and polished and presentable and worthy for. there is only unfettered uninhibited unrestrained unchained care for you here. keep shining as you shine)your light can never dim(all the words and all the feels and all the things you need to fill complete)you are already complete(is already given. is already written. is already yours. is already you. what a great soul inside you. what great energy you carry around you. what a blessing you are. what a blessing. you. are. joy. a joy. a peacful piecefull joy. all that burden and insecurity and heaviness that lingers isn't capable of containing you. always here for you. in the quiet. in the loud. in moments signs tend to show up so you know you are loved for who you are. for how you are. for why you are. keep me on your lips. forever wherever you are. asé.

old soul love.

you are that old soul love. a gentle foundation with deep roots to a time forgotten. a simpler time. when poetry meant something and every word melted onto bone and became part of your being. handwritten notes you note still carry such meaning. such solace your print creates. those poems even though you don't call them poems are birds in flight that nestle and flap and land and stay in hand in hearts in drawers and boxes and carriers and favorite keepsakes to bookmark to remember what your love embers and fragrances on skin. that playlist you cater for special someone's for special occasions for special moments is the tone. sets the tone. that no one does anymore. the thought behind your language that personalizes the kind of velvet your person needs to feel seen. the off the grid desire to just drop from screens drop from gps drop from how to get a hold of and just be present to the analog to the nature to the self to the inner to the more important than others knowing where you are and who you are with all the time. the vinyls you spin to the oils you select to the vines you grow to the attire you rock you are always intentional with the stuff you collect so that it syncs with your vibe. intimacy from an old soul such as you is sacred and serene. so sacred. so serene. love from you)oh you(is soul recognition. is craved. is craved. is craved. because you know the old ways of healing. the old ways of feeling. the old ways of seeing. just by cutting through the surface and superficial that it leaves a forever mark that will never leave never fade never wash. old soul love)you old soul love(cannot go extinct. cannot extinguish. cannot exit. you are a forever water basin that good and beautiful things bloom from. your old soul love is life old soul. your old soul love is necessary old soul. your old soul love is inspirational old soul. your old soul love is magic old soul. your old soul love is enough old soul. your old soul love is everything all at once old soul.

don't forget to breathe.

sometimes you hold yourself in and forget to breathe.

make more waves.

all about you are situations where you constantly scan to say what you know is expected to be heard so you do the thing that causes ease causes no strain but it strains you. it strains you. it pains you. it pricks you. even if you passive aggressive it isn't fully what it is you need to get out or feel will be understood. the call in the beginning entry was to make waves. so the final call will be to make more waves. collapse into whatever it is that you fear and be that. be all of that. take that hesitation and turn it into the beautiful vulnerability you already are and expand. expand. expand. and when you pull yourself back and unpack how it went down you will have nothing to wish you would have done because you did it. say what needs to be said. do what needs to be done. gather yourself to the edge and become the edge become what you are becoming and give everything you give to the world to yourself. give everything you give the world to yourself. daily. this secondly. unapologetically. promise yourself you won't allow yourself to go on empty again and notice more quickly when you're watering dried up wells and allowing takers to pull from your bottomless well and stop yourself from self limiting thoughts and bouts of feeling like you're doing enough or being enough and step away from ideas that no matter how much you give you have to give so much more to prove your love prove your value prove your belonging. believe and know that your ancestors are proud of you grinning for you shouldering you. you change the culture. you are a lighthouse mixed with horizon and troposphere. the greatest hearing and the sky the unlucky ones can't see. you. beloved. are a giver by nature and anything from nature is an always blessing. you are a blessing. so rewind these words these mantras these verses these reminders and mirror you. tell you what you see. what you've always seen but looked away)don't look away anymore(. youmore. youmore. because youmore is what the world needs more of. asante sana for the water you are.

your aura was intended to receive this book as a mirror. did you see your reflection. did you see yourself in a line in a gap in a feeling that welcomed you. i hope so. i hope so. did it help you understand another and the light they give. to press upon them more love better love deeper love. i hope so. i hope so. either way take these with you bestow them to someone breathe these in as often as you want as often as you can. thankful for your giving. thank you dear giver.

xo. adrian michael
text me - 303.529.2197
for words you didn't know   **i appreciate you** 🌹
you needed to hear.
to share anything
that resonated
with you.

Made in the USA
Columbia, SC
26 August 2021